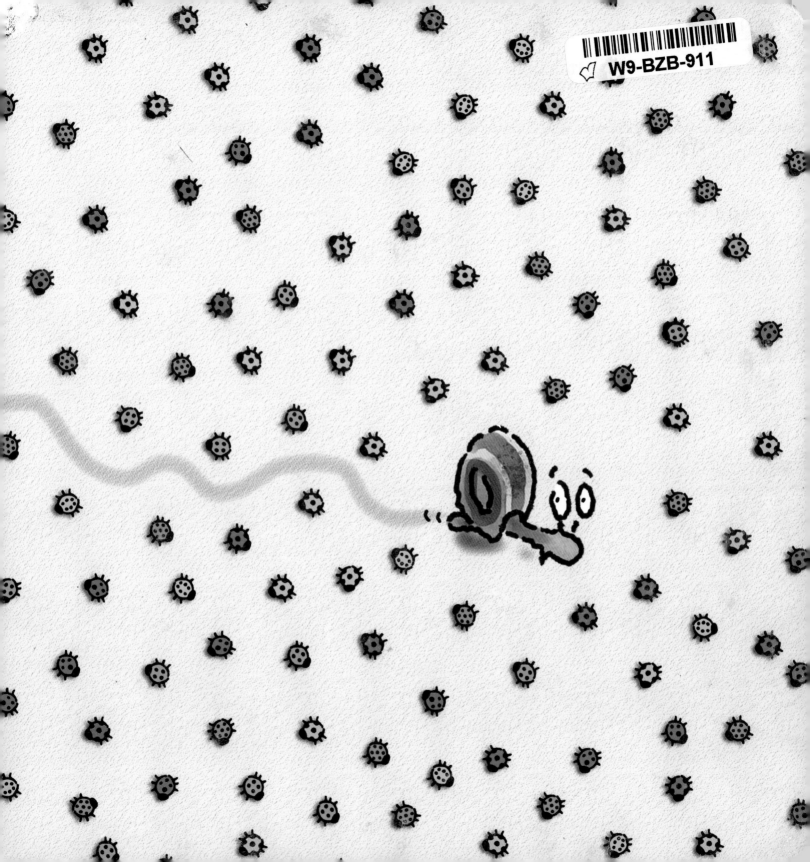

Snug as a Bug?

by **Amy Imbody**
Illustrated by **Mike Gordon**

Zonder**kidz**

The Children's Group of Zondervan Publishing House

Tonight would you like to sleep like a snail,
Slimy and snug in the garden pail?

Well, no, I don't think so. It wouldn't go well
Trying to curl myself into a shell.

Perhaps then you'd rather sleep like a bear
Under the snow in a rocky lair,
Spending six long months in a cave with your brother
Trying not to bump into each other?

No, thank you. I think it'd be a bit tight.
Six months in close quarters could lead to a fight!

Then how would you like to sleep like a shark,
Eyes open wide in the ocean dark?

Or like a parrotfish in its odd bed
Of bubbles it blows all around its green head?
Do you think that'd be fun?
No?

I don't either,
But how would you like to sleep like a beaver?
Just chew a few birch logs and pile them together.
Then you'd sleep cozy through all kinds of weather.

If that sort of bed doesn't sound too appealing,
Then sleep like a fly upside down on the ceiling.

Or sleep like a frog under mud by the lake,
Or under dry leaves in the woods like a snake.

Dear Mother, I know this may sound rather wild,
But tonight I'd prefer just to sleep like a child.

Oh, really?
You mean, right here in your bed?
With sheets and blankets and pillows instead?

Well, my dear, then close your eyes,
And we will pray to the Lord who is wise
And thank him for making you

Not a snail, not a bear, not a shark, not a frog,
Not a beaver, not a fly, not a snake on a log,

But tucked in so tight with a kiss and a hug,
his own little child just as snug as a bug.

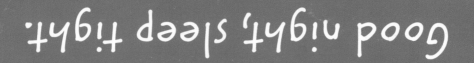

Good night sleep tight.

Mom's Moment

Do you ever wonder what life would be like if you were someone else—the witty celebrity on the television talk show, or the graceful Olympic ice skater, or the near perfect mother down the street? Did you know that God uniquely created you just the way you are for his purposes, and you are making a lasting difference in the world around you? Snuggle down into the comforting truth of that promise as you go to bed tonight.
Good night.

For you created my inmost being;
you knit me together in my mother's womb.
Psalm 139:13

〰

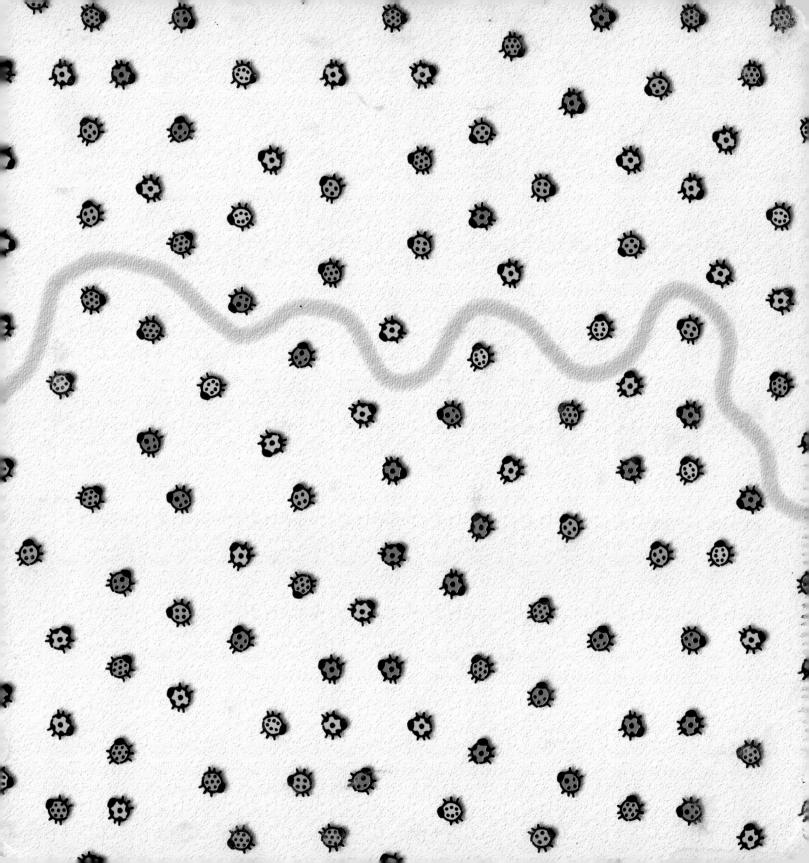